About the Book

The empty lot next to school was covered with weeds. That didn't stop Lincoln from dreaming of a country garden. If he were class president, perhaps everyone could grow tomatoes and pumpkins. They'd make jack-o'-lanterns for Halloween!

But when Lincoln tossed his hat in the ring in the class election, he didn't expect to be called "pumpkin farmer." And he certainly didn't expect to come face to face with criminals when he and his friends tried to find the empty lot's owner!

Here is another exciting—and funny—episode in the life of the popular hero of Plum Street. With lively pictures by Paul Galdone, the book will be a welcome event for all Lincoln fans.

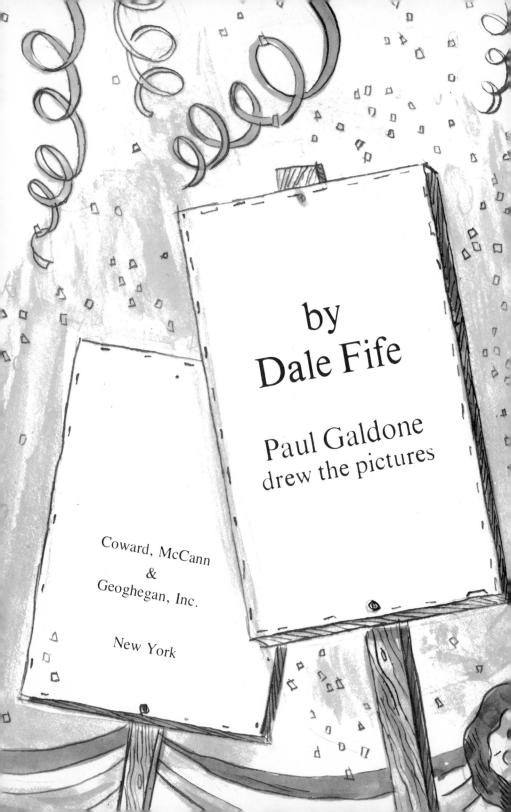

by
Dale Fife

Paul Galdone
drew the pictures

Coward, McCann
&
Geoghegan, Inc.

New York

Library of Congress Cataloging in Publication Data

Fife, Dale.
Who'll vote for Lincoln?
SUMMARY: Lincoln, a candidate for class president,
makes a campaign promise opposed by a group of criminals.
[1. School stories]   I. Galdone, Paul. II. Title.
PZ7.F4793Wgw   [Fic]   76-57127

SBN: 698-30665-1 lib. bdg.
Printed in the United States of America

To John Matteson

1

If Lincoln had not dreamed up the idea of a class garden on the empty lot next to school, and if his favorite uncle had not run for city councilman, he probably never would have gone into politics. In that case, he wouldn't have fallen smack into a ''pork barrel.''

It was Saturday. Suppertime. Pepperoni pizza time. Uncle Jay bought three huge ones on the way home from bowling with Lincoln and Pop.

The good smells of cheese, tomato and sausage rolled around the kitchen and wafted into the dining room.

''Sassy, Sissy,'' Lincoln shouted for the third time, ''when are you going to set the table?''

The middle-sized twins were busy arranging a bunch of early spring crocus in an empty jelly jar on the table. Aunt Charlotte had brought the flowers.

"Call us by our right names," Sassy, the know-it-all twin, said, giving Lincoln a shove.

His sisters were getting to be too much. Now he was supposed to call them Shirley and Sandra.

"We made brownies for dessert. What did you do?" Sissy asked.

"Okay, Silly and Stupid," Lincoln said and grabbed a stack of plates from the sideboard. He pretended they were bowling balls and began to slide them across the table. One glanced off the jelly jar. The flowers slid to the table's edge and teetered there.

Sissy screeched.

Sassy raced around the table to grab the flowers in the nick of time.

"Throttle down," Sara, Lincoln's big sister, bossed from the living room. "Uncle Jay's telling us about next week's special election. It's exciting having someone in the family in politics."

Lincoln hurriedly finished setting the table so that he could stand beside Uncle Jay, his idol.

"I'm not *in* yet," Uncle Jay said. "When I tossed my hat in the ring for the city councilman vacancy, I expected tough opposition."

Aunt Charlotte, who was nervous as a fly buzzing a windowpane, shuddered. "I don't like you running against Sam Watson."

Pop chuckled. "Down at the railroad we call him 'Slippery Sam.' "

"Pizza's on," Mom called, setting two steaming platters on the table.

Lincoln pulled Baby Herman from under the tunnel he had made of the rug and set him in his high chair. Baby Herman swatted Lincoln over the head with his plate. Then gave him a wet kiss.

Pop tossed the salad. "I remember way back we had a candidate for mayor who promised a chicken in every pot. What are you promising, Jay?"

Uncle Jay helped himself to two wedges of pizza. "Excellence," he said.

"What's that mean?" Lincoln asked.

Uncle Jay waggled his fork at Lincoln. "Now there's a boy, my own nephew, growing up with no acquaintance with the forgotten virtue. The way I see it, *excellence* in government means to give the best you've got. To do it *right*."

Pop made a ceremony of grinding pepper over the salad. "All we got from that mayor who promised us all that chicken was a mouthful of feathers."

"They must have tickled going down," Uncle Jay said.

Lincoln grinned across the table at his uncle. The word "excellence" fitted him like a baseball glove. Some day, when Lincoln had time, he'd figure out just how to be like him. Right now, he was in a hurry to meet his Plum Street friends. He ate six wedges of pizza in nothing flat and rushed outside.

2

Wilbur, who lived across the hall from Lincoln, was sitting on the stoop showing Bunky a magic trick. "The hand is quicker than the eye," Wilbur said. He held up his two fists. "Now you see it, now you don't. Which one has the red ball?"

"The left," Bunky said promptly.

Bunky Hanson was little, but he was smart.

Wilbur sagged. "How did you guess?"

"Because my eye is faster than your knobby fist," Bunky said.

"It looks easy when my brother Roscoe does it," Wilbur said.

"Practice. You have to practice," Lincoln said. "Practice for excellence." *"Excellence!"* He liked the sound of the word. *"Excellence!"* It rolled around his mouth smooth as a jawbreaker.

"Hands" Jacks, the big kid with the oversize mitts, who was the best athlete on Plum Street, barged along just in time to hear Lincoln on "excellence."

"What's with this excellence?" he asked.

"Excellence is kind of like shakes made with real ice cream, hot dogs without filler. Nothing phony. It's my uncle's slogan. He's into politics."

Wilbur juggled the red balls. "We're going into politics at school. Ms. Rowe said we'd have a class election."

"Yeah," Hands said. "She wants us to know about election campaigns, how they're conducted. We're gonna have a president and a vice-president, and all the rest."

Ms. Rowe taught social studies. She was also Home Room teacher.

Bunky nosed in. "From what I hear about your class, Mooch will run things no matter what."

Mooch's name was really Booch. Bill Booch. The kids called him "Mooch" because that's what he did. He mooched candy bars, apples, all sorts of things. He was so big and mean, the kids went along with just about everything he or his gang said.

Lincoln straddled the fire plug. "School's no fun since Mooch moved this side of town. There's no class spirit. But maybe if we elected class officers, and had a good president."

"Maybe what?" Hands asked.

"Well, now if I were president . . . ."

"Yeah! What would you do?" Hands asked.

Lincoln sniffed the spring air. He looked up at a fleecy cloud floating by. He thought about his pet project—a country garden in the city, where the kids in his class could grow vegetables and flowers. Most lived in apartments.

"Okay, Link. We're waiting," Hands said. "How would things be different if you were president?"

"Maybe people would listen to me."

"About what?"

"That empty ground next to our school. When I go around asking who the owner is, all I get is the brush off, or a pat on the head. But the president of the class would have authority."

Wilbur pulled a crumpled packet from the pocket of his jeans. "Yeah, I remember, you told Hands and Bunky and me about it, and how easy it would be to grow pumpkins. So I sent for these seeds. They'll be worn out if I don't get them planted."

Bunky nosed into the conversation. "Link, why don't you run for president?"

Hands groaned. "Bunky, you're not in our class, but you ought to know Mooch and his rat pack as well as we do. He yells. The pack jumps."

Bunky stuck out his chin. "Link isn't afraid of anybody."

Wilbur stopped juggling. He looked Lincoln in the eye. "You haven't got the nerve."

"Who says?" Lincoln retorted.

"I says," Wilbur snapped back.

Lincoln got a reckless feeling. "Okay. I'll throw my hat in the ring."

"You haven't got a hat," Wilbur said.

Hands grabbed the lid off the garbage pail and held it over Lincoln's head. "Now he has."

"I'll make posters for you," Bunky offered.

"I'll put them up all around the school," Wilbur said.

Hands strutted importantly. "I'll be your campaign manager."

"Rah! Rah!" Wilbur shouted.

Sissy and Sassy stuck their heads out the front window. "What's up?" Sissy asked.

Hands grinned at the twins. "Your brother's going to be famous. He's going to run for class president."

"Ha!" Sassy snorted. "He'd better start working on his personality."

"That's a big job," Sissy said.

Lincoln bounced up the steps. "What's wrong with my personality?"

"You haven't got one. You'll have to work at developing one. In politics you've got to sort of stick out. You could be the candidate that pets people's dogs or feeds their turtles. Anything to make people remember you when they vote."

Wilbur did a head stand. "I heard of a politician who stood on his head in the lobby of the Sheraton."

"Well, all I'll stand on is *excellence*," Lincoln said.

"You'll need more than that," Hands said. "Ms. Rowe said anyone who wanted to run had to have ten signatures from kids in the class. And that's just to be nominated."

Lincoln grinned. "That's your problem. You're my campaign manager."

Hands made as if to tear out his hair. "Ms. Rowe said to have them in by Monday. Why did I ever get into politics?"

3

It was almost time for class to let out and Ms. Rowe hadn't got to the elections. Lincoln squirmed in his seat while Ms. Rowe, bracelets jangling, straightened her desk.

The class was noisy. Mooch threw a spitball at his Cousin Ruff. Ruff was pulling the hair of Rosa Rush who sat in front of him. Rosa looked mad enough to hit him.

"Simmer down," Ms. Rowe said.

Most of the kids behaved immediately, but, as usual, it took Mooch and Ruff a little longer.

Ms. Rowe pulled her horn-rimmed glasses down on her nose. She consulted a little heap of slips. She frowned. "The nominations turned in for the various class officers are not what I had hoped for." She stood and transferred the names onto the chalkboard.

When she got to "President" she turned to the class. "I have just one nomination for this office. The chalk squeaked as she wrote: LINCOLN FARNUM.

Mooch turned around to Lincoln. "Yuk!" he said.

"Yuk! Yuk!" Ruff mimicked.

Some of the kids tittered.

Ms. Rowe rapped for attention. "I had hoped for a serious, exciting campaign. I've decided to give you an extra day to bring in further nominations."

The bell rang. The kids filed out. Hands and Wilbur joined up with Lincoln in the hall. "You don't need a campaign manager to run against yourself," Hands said. "You'll win by a landslide."

"I kind of hoped for a knock-down-drag-em-out fight," Wilbur said.

Bunky was waiting at the school entrance. "How many kids running for president?" he asked.

"One. Me," Lincoln said.

"That's good," Bunky said.

"No, it's bad," Lincoln said. "Means the kids aren't much interested."

"Not all bad," Hands said. "That way you'll be sure to be elected, and we'll have a better chance to get that garden. I hope no one else runs."

Lincoln headed in the direction of the lot. "Let's look it over."

When they reached the lot, there was Officer Roberts. He jotted something down in his notebook. He greeted them and went on.

Hands pulled up a handful of weeds. "Where's the best place to plant tomatoes? I want the big beefsteak kind."

"In the sunniest part," Lincoln said. "I read that in the garden column of the newspaper."

"Sweet corn's another thing I want to plant," Hands said.

"Hey, leave some space for pumpkins," Wilbur said.

"Who said I wanted pumpkins?" Hands asked.

"Everybody in the class wants a pumpkin, right Link?" Wilbur said.

Lincoln grinned. "On Halloween they do." He scanned the lot. "First thing we should do is measure the ground. Step it off to see how much of a plot each person can have."

The lot was wedged in between the bank and the school. It ended in a thick stand of thorn bushes along a high board fence. Until a year ago a dilapidated building had stood on it. That had been bulldozed down. Now it was rank with weeds.

Lincoln planted himself, feet apart, on the lot. He imagined he was a surveyor squinting through a telescope. "Bunky, you step off the rear of the property."

"Okay," Bunky said. He rushed through the weeds, so high that soon he was hidden from sight.

"Wilbur and Hands, you two do the sidelines," Lincoln said. "I'll measure off the front."

Before they could get started they heard Bunky's yell. "Help! The bushes got me."

"Hang in there," Lincoln called.

The three boys ran to the back of the lot. Bunky was hanging in there all right. The thorny bushes had ahold of his pants and a grip on his shirt. The boys laughed as they pried him loose.

"How did you manage to get yourself hung up like this?" Lincoln asked.

"I was hiding from the man. I wondered what he was up to. Where'd he go?"

"What man?" Lincoln asked.

"Didn't you see him? A sporty guy in a checked jacket and plaid cap. He was standing right by the bushes here, looking over the weeds, watching you guys. I thought you'd see him."

Wilbur, Lincoln and Hands looked at one another. No one had seen the man in the plaid cap.

"He couldn't just disappear," Bunky said.

"What did he look like?" Lincoln asked.

"I couldn't see his face because of the cap," Bunky said.

"He must be somewhere," Lincoln said. "What's on the other side of this fence?"

"It used to be Madam Zodiac, Fortune Teller. Now it's a church. But there's no way through the thorny bushes."

An idea struck Lincoln. "Maybe the preacher of that church knows something about this lot since the church backs up to it. Let's go around and see."

The four of them scooted around the bank corner, and over onto Plum Street to the rickety building. The sign over the door said CHURCH OF THE LAST CHANCE.

"The preacher in our church likes company," Lincoln said, and he walked right up to the door and knocked.

A mini slot in the door opened up. An eye and a bushy eyebrow peeked out. "No services today," a pious voice said. The slot closed.

"It's spooky," Wilbur said. "Let's go."

"I didn't get a chance to ask about the lot," Lincoln said. He knocked again.

The slot opened a crack.

"I'm Lincoln Farnum. I go to the school around the block. So do my friends here. I'm trying to find out who owns the lot back of your church. It would be a great place for a class garden."

The eyebrow rose. It twitched. "You mean a group of kids want to dig all around and bother my parishioners?"

"There's that high fence and the thorn bushes in between," Lincoln said. "We won't be any trouble . . . ."

The door snapped shut.

"Not very polite for a preacher," Hands said.

"He's right though," said Bunky. "If Mooch and some of his gang started whooping it up on the lot, they could disturb prayers. Let's go."

Lincoln hesitated. "Let's look around the back." He started for the rear of the building. He tried to peek into the back window of the church but there was a dark curtain over it.

Hands counted six cases of empty bottles stacked against the back fence. "Looks like they had a church festival," he said.

Lincoln inspected the high board fence that separated the church from the vacant lot. "Say, isn't this kind of a gate?" He pushed at a loose looking panel. It swung out easily into a space that had been pruned out of the thick thorn bushes. They walked through the tunnel-like opening. They were back on the lot.

"Who'd have guessed you could walk through like that," Wilbur said.

From this angle, the lot looked large. Wide. Lincoln began to dream again. He saw rows of lettuce, poles of string beans. He saw bright pumpkins—dozens of them—enough so everyone in the class could have a jack-o'-lantern come next Halloween. He saw the whole city travelling to Plum Street to see the lighted pumpkins in the apartment windows. Plum Street, his school, would be special.

Bunky punctured his dream. "The man I saw in the plaid cap was probably on his way through the thorn bushes to say his prayers. That's why the preacher doesn't want a garden here. It's a short cut from the street through the lot to the church."

"I guess you're right," Lincoln said.

The pumpkins vanished. The lot was just a mess of old weeds.

4

Lincoln's name was still the only one on the chalk-board under "President" when he got to Social Studies the next day.

Ms. Rowe's earrings moved like tiny swings as she called for order. "Do we have any more nominations for class officers?" she asked.

Mooch's cousin, Ruff, chewing a mouthful of something, lumbered up the aisle and handed Ms. Rowe a slip of paper.

Ms. Rowe adjusted her glasses. "We have another candidate for president," she said and turned to the chalk-board.

Lincoln hoped it would be Rosa Rush. She would give him a rousing run for it.

It was Mooch.

Mooch!!

Why?

He never did anything good for the class. He was smart enough, but he did just enough work to get passing grades.

Ms. Rowe turned back to the class. "Each candidate will now state his platform."

When it came to the office of president, she motioned to Lincoln to go first.

Lincoln had thought it all out. He knew exactly what he wanted to say. He had talked it over with Uncle Jay, with Mom and Pop, even Sara.

"I'm not promising anything," Lincoln began. "I'm asking for things. I'm asking everyone in the class to work with me for *excellence*—excellence in school government, like appointing committees to get things done. We ought to begin by seeing the room is kept clean, by keeping the plants watered, taking care of what we've got. Then we want excellence in school work. If we all pull together, we'll get back *excellence* in school spirit. We'll be one up. My platform is one word: *Excellence*."

There was scattered applause.

Wilbur held up his package of pumpkin seeds. "You said if you were president you'd see we had a class garden and everyone could have a pumpkin for Halloween."

"Yeah," Hands chimed in. "How about the tomatoes and corn you said I could raise on the lot next door?"

The class came to life.

The room buzzed. "Let's plant nasturtiums . . . . I like daisies . . . . How about peas? Pumpkin, pumpkin, we all want a pumpkin. . . ."

Lincoln quieted them. "What I said was that the class president would stand a better chance of being listened to, and finding out who owns the lot. If we got permission to use it, that would be *excellent*."

As he sat down, Lincoln felt a little uneasy about having the lot mentioned when he really did not know how to go about getting it.

Ms. Rowe motioned Mooch to the front of the room.

Mooch always strode as if he owned the world with a barbed-wire fence wrapped around it. His bold smile showed a mouthful of big teeth. He stood in front of the class with his feet wide apart, hands on hips. His big arm muscles bulged through his T-shirt. "I say we need some changes around here," he shouted.

"You tell 'em," his cousin Ruff yelled.

"Now I've got a platform that means something,"
Mooch went on. "Ready for it?" He raised a fist. *"Bigger Is Better!"*

"Exactly what does that mean?" Rosa popped up to
ask.

"What it says. Bigger and better everything. Are you tired of skinny hot dogs and no fries in the cafeteria?"

"Natch," someone yelled.

"Would you like double-dip ice cream cones for the price you're paying for one dip? And how about longer recess periods, less homework, and more school holidays?"

"Yeah!" the kids yelled. Even Wilbur joined in, until Hands threw a paper clip at him.

"Then I'm your man," Mooch cried.

He returned to his seat to the noise of his gang pounding on their desks.

Rosa raised her hand. "In regular elections, there is always a Gallup poll to see how the voting is going to go. May we have one?"

"Good idea, Rosa," Ms. Rowe said. "How about you chairing it? The candidates will campaign, and then on Thursday, the day before our elections, you can give us the results of the poll."

Lincoln felt a prickle of excitement. The election began to seem professional. Just like the national ones on TV. Rosa was smart. She'd handle the poll fairly.

Still, he was bothered about Mooch. He didn't like school. Why was he running for president? Lincoln was still wondering when the bell rang.

"There goes our next president," Wilbur said to Lincoln as the classroom emptied and Mooch strutted on ahead of them. "Did you hear the great things he promised?"

"Promised!" Lincoln exploded. "He didn't promise a thing. He just asked if we'd like those things."

"Say, you're right," Wilbur said. "It was an optical illusion."

"You mean a brainwash," Hands, who had joined them, said.

"Double-talk," Lincoln said. "The kids all know Mooch. They won't be taken in."

Hands stuffed his big mitts into the pockets of his jeans. "Don't be too sure. Besides, he's got his rat pack. As your campaign manager, I say it's time to do something zaptacular."

"Bunky offered to do a poster," Lincoln said.

"Have him get some zip into it," Hands said. "Something like this: IF YOU VOTE FOR MOOCH, THE MOOCHER, HIS RAT PACK WILL GET THE CHEESE, AND YOU'LL BE IN THE TRAP.

"WOW!" Wilbur said. "That's great. Bunky can draw a picture of the school building caught in a rat trap, and show Mooch with a rat's face gnawing at it."

Lincoln drifted toward home. "I don't want a smear campaign."

Hands kept step. "What other kind is there?"

Wilbur jogged along. "I've got an idea. Make bigger and better promises than Mooch."

Lincoln chuckled. "That would have to be free trips to the moon, and who's got a rocket? I want a dignified campaign. How about a poster showing our school flying a flag with the one word 'EXCELLENCE' and below it: 'Shake the hand of Lincoln Farnum.' "?

Hands shrugged. "It's got more sag than zap."

"It's not earsplitting," Wilbur said.

"You mean 'eye-catching,' " Hands said.

"It says what I stand for," Lincoln said.

"Yeah, but you also stand for a garden," Hands said. It should read: 'Shake the hand of the Pumpkin Farmer.' Let's get Bunky to do the sign right away, so the kids will see it first thing in the morning."

They had come alongside the empty lot. Lincoln was the first to see the new sign:

KEEP OFF. PRIVATE PROPERTY. THIS MEANS YOU.

His heart sank.

"Does 'you' mean us?" Wilbur asked.

"Looks like it," Lincoln said. "I wonder who put it

up. Could be the preacher. He wasn't friendly.''

Hands' jaw sagged. ''Maybe the owner.''

Wilbur picked up a rock and threw it at the sign.

Hands kicked at some weeds. ''I just sent for a seed catalog.''

Wilbur picked up another rock and threw it at the sign. It toppled over.

That was what was happening to his hopes for a country garden, Lincoln thought. They were toppling.

Were?

Had!

5

"What's the big hurry?" Wilbur asked the next morning as he tried to keep up with Lincoln.

"I want to hear what the kids at school say about the poster," Lincoln shouted over his shoulder.

They skidded to a stop at the corner of the school building where Bunky and Hands were slumped against a tree stump. Bunky pointed to a poster strung across the entrance to the school. It was so huge it made Lincoln's poster fade into nothing.

The big poster read:

EXSSELLANCE IS ONE OF THOUSANDS OF WORDS IN
THE DICTIONARY. THERE IS ONLY ONE MOOCH.
DON'T VOTE FOR A DEAD WORD.
VOTE FOR A LIVE ONE—MOOCH! MOOCH! MOOCH!

Wilbur let out a whistle. "The guy really says something."

"What?" Lincoln demanded. "And he doesn't even know how to spell *Excellence*."

Hands stuck his mitts in his pockets. "As your campaign manager, I say it's time to take off the kid gloves."

"What does that mean?" Wilbur asked.

Hands doubled his fists and danced around Wilbur, getting a punch in here, one there. "We've got to find Mooch's weak point."

"That's easy," Bunky said. "His brain."

"Yeah, it's filled with sawdust," Hands said.

Bunky did a handspring. "WOW! That gives me an idea for a really great poster."

"It better have some zap this time," Hands said. "The rally's tomorrow. We need something to juice up our campaign before Rosa takes the poll."

They got it.

Even Hands howled when he saw the poster. It showed

Mooch's head filled with sawdust which trickled out of one ear as fast as his cousin Ruff poured more into the other ear. The balloon over Mooch's head read:

"HELP! HOW DO YOU SPELL EXSELLENSE?"

In one corner Bunky had drawn a caricature of Lincoln as a wise owl, dictionary under his arm, saying: "Mooch doesn't know how to spell what I'm running for. Now One More Time: E X C E L L E N C E ."

They laughed as they tacked it to the outdoor bulletin board just as it was beginning to get dark.

They laughed all the way to school the next morning. Until they got there. Mooch was the center of a crowd of students. He was handing out peanuts from a big box. "Free peanuts," he yelled. "Come and get your free peanuts while they last."

Ruff walked up and down the school yard wearing a sandwich poster. It read:

PEANUTS ARE GOOD TO EAT. BUT DON'T VOTE FOR
ONE.
VOTE FOR BIGGER IS BETTER. VOTE FOR MOOCH FOR
PRESIDENT.

"I didn't think Mooch had enough brains to write anything," Lincoln said.

"Maybe he's got a speechwriter," Bunky said. "I

heard even presidents of the United States usually do.''

A van drove up to the school entrance.

''The peanut man's back,'' someone yelled.

Mooch ran to the van. The driver handed him another big box of peanuts.

"Who's that?" Lincoln asked.

Bunky moved in closer to the van to get a better look at the driver.

Kids swarmed around it. They stuffed peanuts into their pockets and book bags. Even Wilbur was chewing a mouthful.

"We'd better caucus," Hands said.

They huddled.

Wilbur had bad news. "They say everyone on the baseball team's gonna vote for Mooch."

"How about the girls?" Lincoln asked.

Just then a group of girls came along. One of them threw a peanut at Lincoln. The others followed suit. It rained peanuts.

"Well, I guess that answers your question," Hands said. "Link, you've got to come up with something brilliant.

Lincoln thought and thought. His brain seemed to be on vacation. He couldn't come up with a single new idea.

Mooch was still surrounded by a crowd of peanut crunching kids.

"Speech! Speech!" Ruff yelled.

"Speech! Speech!" Mooch's gang cried.

"Speech!" the kids mimicked through mouthfuls of peanuts.

Mooch jumped up on a trash can and shook hands with himself over his head. "My fellow students," he shouted, "I hope you all enjoyed the BIGGER IS BET-TER goobers. They're just a sample of what's coming if you vote for me tomorrow. Now my opponent is campaigning on *excellence*. I ask you, have you ever tried to eat a mouthful of excellence?"

"Yeah!" Ruff yelled. "It's chock-full of nothing."

The kids laughed.

"My opponent talks about a country garden," Mooch went on. "Where is it you ask? Why, it's right next door. You can see it anytime you want. It's filled with *excellence*. The most excellent weeds in the whole city. And that's what you'll get if you vote for the old Pumpkin

Farmer. Anyone for more peanuts?''

He tossed the rest of the peanuts from the box and jumped off the trash can.

Hands gave Lincoln a shove toward the front of the crowd. "*Say* something. You gotta say *something*."

Lincoln didn't know what.

"Get on with it," Hands said. "It's your last chance."

Lincoln stood in a pool of peanut shells. He ground them with his shoes. "Mooch gives you peanuts," he said finally. "And that's exactly what he'll give you as president. Peanuts!"

"What you going to give us?" someone yelled.

"Handshakes," one of Mooch's gang shouted. "We can't eat handshakes."

A girl shouted. "How about a choc shake. We could eat that."

"CHOC SHAKES, CHOC SHAKES, WE WANT CHOC SHAKES," someone cried.

The kids took up the chant:

"CHOC SHAKES, CHOC SHAKES, CHOC SHAKES, CHOC SHAKES."

The sort of jeering good humor, his will to be president, the rhythm of the shouting, got to Lincoln. He saw himself blown up big as a giant, handing choc shakes all around.

"'Okay!'' he shouted. "If I'm elected, everyone in the class gets a choc shake.''

"Lincoln. We want Lincoln,'' Hands shouted.

The kids took up the cry.

The bell rang.

Lincoln's feet didn't seem to touch the ground as he walked to the classroom and took his seat. It was a wonderful feeling.

And now for the poll.

He watched Rosa go up to the front of the room. She looked at the paper in her hand. Would she ever get with it? She was delaying on purpose.

She looked straight at Lincoln, eyes teasing. "According to the poll, twenty-five percent of the class say . . .''

Lincoln's heart sank . . . he'd lost . . .

"twenty-five percent of the class say Mooch. Seventy-five percent say Lincoln!''

Hands bounded to Lincoln's desk. "We're in,'' he shouted over the hubbub.

Lincoln tried to hide his elation. "I'm not elected yet.''

"Mooch hasn't got a chance,'' Hands said. "The kids have finished his peanuts. They'll vote for the choc shakes.''

6

Lincoln could hardly wait for school to be out so he could tell his family about the poll. He ran all the way home.

Mom was at the stove when he skidded down the hall and into the kitchen.

"When I left this morning, I was just an ordinary kid," Lincoln announced. "Now the poll says I've got a seventy-five percent chance of being president."

Mom gave him a hug. "That calls for a celebration."

It was then that Lincoln saw Uncle Jay. He was sitting quietly at the kitchen table drinking a mug of coffee. "Looks like I should have taken lessons in politics from you, Link. Maybe I wouldn't have lost."

Uncle Jay lose the election? Lincoln couldn't believe it. "How? Why?" he asked.

"My opponent promised great things," Uncle Jay said.

Mom lifted the ladle from the stew and shook it. "That scoundrel. He bought those votes. He can't deliver what he promised."

Uncle Jay got to his feet. "Yes, but he's in and I'm out. Well, it's time to go home."

He shook hands with Lincoln. "Congratulations. I know you'll win fair and square."

Mom followed Uncle Jay to the door. Lincoln stood looking out the kitchen window down at the cement square below. He could see the basketball net Uncle Jay had put up for him. He remembered how Uncle Jay, a star player in college, had taught him the fine points of the game. Uncle Jay was a real star. The best. EXCELLENT was the word for him.

Mom came back into the kitchen. "Anything wrong, son? Seems you should be shouting about."

"Nothing," he said and bolted to his room.

He sat on the edge of his bed and had this awful cold feeling in his stomach. He had done something Uncle Jay would not do. He had promised shakes for votes. He figured:

36 Shakes. 36 × 60¢ = $21.60.

He reached for his bank and shook it until all the coins dropped out. The pile didn't seem very big. He counted: $4.57.

That would buy only about seven and a half shakes.

The cold feeling in his stomach got stronger. He had not only made a big election promise, he couldn't keep it.

Mom called from the kitchen, "Mind running down to the super?"

Lincoln dragged himself to the kitchen and took the two quarters Mom handed him. "I need powdered sugar to frost a special cake for a special event," she said, eyes smiling.

Lincoln forced his lips into a grin. He turned the quarters over in his hand. Fifty cents. It wouldn't buy even one shake. He had to buy thirty-six.

"Mom," he stumbled. "Any way I can earn some money?"

Mom eyed him solemnly. "You've been saving a quarter a week from your allowance. What do you need money for?"

He couldn't tell her.

"Things," he said and rushed from the kitchen.

On the way back from the super he got the idea of going into the drugstore to ask Mr. Woods if he would sell thirty-six shakes wholesale. Maybe even half price.

"Thirty-six shakes," Mr. Woods' voice sounded cracked. "For kids from your school? They'll tear the place apart. If you bring in thirty-six kids for shakes, they'll cost you not sixty cents, but seventy cents apiece. The whole store will be a shambles. The last thing I want . . . ."

Lincoln backed out the door while Mr. Woods was still talking.

Halfway home he bumped into Mrs. Krutznitt. "Need anything from the grocery?" Lincoln asked. Sometimes Mrs. Krutznitt paid him for carting heavy things.

She shook her head. "My pantry is all stocked up," she said. "Have a good day."

A good day!

He dragged on home.

The table was set. Pop was home. Sissy and Sassy were playing a record so loud it hurt Lincoln's ears. He went into his room, closed the door. It was as if he had to be alone to keep his horrible secret from showing.

When Sara called everyone to dinner, Lincoln didn't feel one bit hungry.

"What's going on?" Pop asked, taking his place at the table, eyeing the chocolate cake sitting grandly in the center.

Mom beamed. "We're having a preelection night party, just as they do in big politics. The student poll showed Lincoln would win the election tomorrow by seventy-five percent."

"That's great," Pop said. "But you know the saying about not counting your chickens until they show their feathers."

Sassy took a helping of stew. "Lincoln can't lose."

45

"He's the talk of the school," Sissy said. "But how's he going to pay for all those shakes he promised?

Lincoln wished he could crawl under the table.

Pop's hand, with a forkful of stew, froze in midair.

Mom looked at Lincoln, openmouthed.

Five pairs of eyes stared at him. Six. Even Baby Herman's.

Sara boiled over. "You mean you promised shakes for votes?"

"He couldn't really help it," Sissy said. "Mooch gave peanuts."

"Maybe I won't win," Lincoln croaked.

"With thirty-six kids promised shakes, you can't lose," Sassy said.

"How you going to pay for them?" Pop asked.

Sara glared at Lincoln. "No one keeps campaign promises. Right, Lincoln?"

Lincoln felt he was going to be sick. He practically crawled to his room.

He lay down on his bed.

The last thing he wanted now was to win the election.

But Sassy was right.

How could he lose?

7

Election day.

Lincoln didn't eat breakfast, even though it was cinnamon rolls and cocoa.

He didn't want to see anyone. On his way to school he walked the opposite way around the block so he wouldn't bump into Hands and Wilbur.

The Pizza Parlor was shuttered at this hour, and Mr. Woods was just opening up his drugstore. Officer Roberts was at the corner directing school children across the street. He greeted Lincoln with a little salute, but Lincoln didn't take much notice.

Lincoln crossed the street and walked along the side of the Opera House. When he turned into School Street he saw some of his classmates clustered on the sidewalk. He didn't want to talk so he scooted right on past them to the empty lot.

This morning he didn't dream of rows of golden pumpkins. He saw weeds—WEEDS—W E E D S.

Then he saw Bunky crouched behind a clump of thistles.

"Shh!" Bunky whispered.

Lincoln got down beside him. "What's up?"

Bunky pointed to a man approaching from the far side of the lot near the church. He wore a black suit and black hat. "He came out of nowhere from behind the bushes, just like the one the other day," Bunky said. "He hasn't got on the checked suit and plaid cap, but he could be the same guy. He's the same size. Wish he'd turn around so we could see what he looks like."

"Wonder what he's got in that bag," Lincoln said. "It looks like one of those canvas ones the bank uses."

"Could be he's a kidnapper and he's just picked up a million dollar-ransom," Bunky said.

The man reached the sidewalk, but he turned the other way.

"We'd better follow him" Bunky said. "Get a look at him, so we can identify him."

They slunk into position.

At the corner, the man stopped right in front of the bank.

Lincoln and Bunky dropped behind the mailbox.

"Could be he's a safe blower," Bunky whispered.

They watched as the man approached the bank. Bunky grabbed Lincoln's arm. "Maybe he's got a stick of dynamite."

From the way the man carried the canvas bag, it seemed heavy. He stopped in front of the small steel door set in the wall alongside the bank entrance. He reached for a key from his pocket and put it in the lock.

"What's he doing?" Bunky asked, spelling out the word over the square steel door—" D e p o s i t o r y."

"That's where people put money when the bank is closed," Lincoln said.

They watched the man pull open the door and slide the bag down the chute.

Lincoln poked Bunky in the ribs. "Kidnapper—safe blower. Some detectives we are. He's got to be the preacher from the Church of the Last Chance depositing collection money."

Just then, the man turned around.

"It's the preacher all right," Lincoln said. "I could never forget the bushy eyebrow I saw through the mini door of the church."

"He isn't the preacher," Bunky said.

"What do you mean he isn't the preacher?"

"That's Mooch's uncle."

"Since when do you know Mooch's uncle?"

"Since yesterday. He brought the peanuts for Mooch to give to the kids. I heard Mooch call him uncle."

"Lots of kids call older men uncle. I say he's the preacher."

"You can't tell by an eyebrow," Bunky said.

The man had started toward Plum Street.

"Let's follow and see where he goes," Lincoln said.

They scooted after him and reached the corner just in time to see him disappear through the front door of the Church of the Last Chance.

"So he is the preacher," Lincoln said.

Bunky was obstinate. "He's Mooch's uncle."

Wilbur and Hands came loping along.

Wilbur walloped Lincoln across the shoulders. "You should be out shaking hands and making speeches. This is election day."

"Lincoln's a cinch to win. He doesn't have to do anymore campaigning," Hands said.

Bunky chimed in. "I hear everyone's for you."

"Well, I'm not," Lincoln blurted.

Hands glared at him. "What's that supposed to mean?"

Lincoln blinked. He was filled with misery. He turned and ran to the school and to his classroom.

He was the first one there. He buried his head in a book.

He didn't look up when the kids tramped in. He didn't look up when he heard Ms. Rowe's bracelets jangling and the chalk squeaking. But he heard what she said: "Each candidate has one minute to give a final talk. We'll use this timer."

Lincoln heard the speeches—the would-be secretaries; sergeants at arms; vice-presidents; treasurers.

Then it was time to hear from the presidential nominees. Ms. Rowe asked Mooch to go first.

Lincoln glanced up to see Mooch go up the aisle with his usual swagger. He fixed his gaze on Lincoln. "I'd like to ask just one question about my worthy opponent, the Pumpkin Farmer. What's he worthy of? I'll tell you. He's worthy of making silly talk, like our having a country garden right here in the city. Now he's promised shakes. I ask you, do you really expect ever to taste them?"

The timer tinked.

Now it was Lincoln's turn.

He went up to the front. He looked at the kids. He knew most of them were his friends. He swallowed hard.

"Mooch is right," he began, and his voice sounded as if it were coming through oatmeal. "You won't get the shakes. I can't buy them. I haven't got the money. It wasn't right to bribe for votes. I withdraw my name from nomination."

No one stirred. The class seemed stunned.

Lincoln's eyes felt hot. He started for the door.

"Lincoln, come back," Ms. Rowe called.

He kept on going. Out of the classroom. Out of the school building. He didn't stop until he reached the empty lot. He threw himself down in the weeds. Never again would he enter the doors of that school. Maybe he'd stow away on a tramp steamer for some far-off place and never come home again.

He heard voices close by. He raised up on his elbow.

Two men were crossing the lot, heading in the direction of the thorny bushes.

Right behind them came another.

Lincoln had never been on the lot at this time of day.

The preacher must be having services.

The preacher!

Who was he really?

Lincoln was sure he was the man with the bushy eyebrows who had not wanted the kids to plant a garden. The same man, in preacher's clothes, had put the collection money in the bank. He was certain it was the same man. No two men would have eyebrows like that.

But Bunky insisted that the man was Mooch's uncle, and that he had provided the peanuts for Mooch's rally.

Then there was the man in the checked suit and plaid cap who had spied on the boys in the lot. Who was he?

Plaid Cap!

Lincoln sat bolt upright.

He remembered something. The man who gave Mooch the peanuts had worn a plaid cap.

Was it possible that the preacher, the peanut man, and the man who had spied on them in the lot were one and the same?

Lincoln heard raucous laughter. He craned his neck and saw three more men heading toward the back of the lot.

He scrambled to his feet and followed them.

He followed them right through the gate. Then he hid behind a pile of rubbish and watched.

One of the men knocked on the back door: Knock . . . KNOCK . . . K N O C K!

The door opened.

The men disappeared into the church.

Why didn't they go through the front door, Lincoln wondered.

Two more men came through the gate.

Lincoln slipped out of his hiding place. He walked right behind them.

They knocked three times.

The door opened.

They went inside. And so did Lincoln.

It was a funny church. Dim. Lots of smoke. Crazy

music. Loud talk: "I'll bet ten dollars on Flying Mane in the third. . . ."

Words: "WIN" "SHOW" "PLACE"

Bottles. Glasses. Ice.

Lincoln saw a green felt-topped table with lots of money on it. The men gathered around the table were betting so eagerly that none of them noticed Lincoln.

What was going on? Lincoln felt confused and scared.

Suddenly there was a pounding on the front door. A hush fell over the place.

A man in a checked suit rushed to the door and peeked through the mini opening. He shut it fast. "COP" he mouthed. Lincoln barely managed to scrunch down under the table to get out of the way of the crush as the men pushed out the back door.

What happened next was like a magic show—now you see it, now you don't.

In the blink of an eye, the man in the checked suit pulled on a black robe. Now he looked like a preacher. Lincoln took particular notice of the man's eyebrows. They were bushy.

The music went from loud to soft. Lincoln knew the tune: "Lead Kindly Light."

A curtain fell from the ceiling. It hid the table with the money. Lincoln crawled out from under it just in time to see the preacher open the door.

"Good day, Officer Roberts. How good of you to visit my humble church," the preacher said in a pious voice.

Officer Roberts was Lincoln's friend. He was relieved to see him. This was a weird place, and Lincoln didn't know what to make of it. He dashed for the door.

Officer Roberts did a double take. "Lincoln, what are you doing out of school?"

"I went to church," Lincoln stammered.

Officer Roberts' eyes widened. "To the Church of the Last Chance?"

"Yeah, but it's a funny kind of church."

The preacher seemed to be choking. He finally found his voice. "You better get on back to school." He gave Lincoln a shove. "The truant officer will be after you."

But Officer Roberts blocked his way. "What do you mean 'funny church' "?

"Well, first there were a lot of men here, and they were playing games with money. . . ."

The preacher interrupted. "Boy, you do have a great capacity for telling stories. Come in Officer Roberts. Look for yourself. There is no one here."

"But there was," Lincoln insisted. "When you knocked they all ran out the back door."

Suddenly, Lincoln got the connection. "ZOWIE!" he yelled. "They went through the secret passage in the

hedge and through the empty lot to the other street. It's the same way they came in. I saw them."

"I'll have a look around," Officer Roberts said.

After the "look" things happened fast. In minutes there was a squad car in front. Bushy Eyebrows, alias the preacher, alias the peanut man, alias the plaid cap, got a free ride to the police station.

When it was all over, Officer Roberts locked up the church. Then he shook hands with Lincoln. "You helped me crack the case by giving me information I've been trying to get for sometime. One thing still bothers me. What were you doing here?"

Lincoln told Officer Roberts about his country garden project. "I've been trying to find out who owns the lot next to our school. I thought the preacher might know since the church backs up to it. I guess I'll never find out who owns it. Nobody seems to know."

"I know."

"You do?"

"That's why I'm here," Officer Roberts said. "The absentee landlord, Mr. Biggs—he owns both the lot and the "church" building—contacted the police department. He'd heard rumors that the Church of the Last Chance was a bookie joint."

BOOKIE JOINT. Lincoln knew what that meant.

Officer Roberts went on: "Mr. Biggs will be grateful for the information you gave me."

Lincoln wondered how grateful. He was almost afraid to ask. "Do you think he'd let my class plant a garden?"

Officer Roberts grinned. "The city's been after Mr. Biggs to get rid of the weeds on his lot. Here, I'll write his address down for you. Offer him a good clean-up job in payment for using the lot. When I report to him, I'll tell him how you cracked the case for me. I'm pretty sure he'll be glad to have a fine garden on his lot instead of a fire hazard and a summons."

Lincoln couldn't get back to school fast enough. Now it didn't matter that he was not president.

The class was out for recess. "Hey, Lincoln," Hands shouted as he shot by. Lincoln didn't stop.

He rushed into the school and to his desk. He got out some paper and began the letter:

"Dear Mr. Biggs. . . ."

He had almost finished when the other kids came trooping back to their seats. Suddenly he realized that the room was unusually quiet. He glanced up. Everyone was looking at him. Grinning.

"Speech!" Wilbur cried.

"Speech!" the class echoed.

Lincoln's mouth dropped open. "Who *me*?"

Hands gave him the victory sign. "Yes, Mr. President."

Lincoln was stunned. "I told you I can't buy those shakes," he said.

Rosa turned around and gave him a great smile. "The poll showed we were all going to vote for you before you promised those shakes," she said.

Ms. Rowe nodded approval. "Your admitting that promising the shakes was a no-no proved to the class that you really meant what you said about 'Excellence.' In addition to taking the poll, Rosa and her committee investigated the election promises made. Rosa would you care to report on this?"

Rosa jumped to her feet. She looked right at Mooch as she talked. "We found that most of the promises could not be carried out. We came up with the resolution that in future elections every campaign promise is to be checked out before the election."

"Good," Ms. Rowe said.

Mooch scrunched low in his seat. Lincoln felt a little sorry for him. Mooch fiddled with a piece of paper. He turned around, stuck the paper on a pencil, and waved the "white flag" at Lincoln. "We await your speech, your Excellency," Mooch said.

At that the whole class laughed.

Lincoln grinned. He got to his feet, but he was still so unravelled by all that had happened that his legs felt like limp macaroni.

More than anything he wanted to tell the class the great news about Mr. Biggs and the country garden. But he remembered what Pop had said: "Don't count your chickens until you see their feathers." He'd wait until Mr. Biggs answered his letter.

He opened his mouth, but all that came out at this historic moment in his life was: "Thanks."

He sat down.

The applause sounded sweet in his ears. He felt all warm and thankful and confident.

A slight breeze came through the open window. Lincoln imagined he could hear corn growing, and string beans snapping. He thought he could smell the vines of tomatoes. As for the pumpkins, he imagined it was Halloween. Every window on Plum Street had a jack-o'-lantern.

Lighted, they were an excellent sight indeed.

About the Author

Dale Fife lives in San Mateo, California, where she spends a good deal of time writing. She is the author of both adult and juvenile books. Besides the popular Lincoln titles, her stories for young readers include *Adam's ABC, Ride the Crooked Wind,* and *Walk a Narrow Bridge,* for which she received the juvenile award of the Martha Kinney Cooper Ohioana Library Association in 1967.

About the Artist

Paul Galdone has illustrated over 100 books for young readers, including the four previous Lincoln books. He has twice been runner-up for the Caldecott award.

The artist divides his time between his home in Rockland County, New York, and his farm in Vermont.